Published in 2017 by Simply Read Books
www.simplyreadbooks.com
Text & illustrations © 2013 Satoe Tone

LIBRARY AND ARCHIVES CANADA CATALOGUING IN PUBLICATION

Tone, Satoe
[Dove batte il cuore. English]
Where the heart is / written and illustrated by Satoe Tone.

Translation of: Dove batte il cuore.
ISBN 978-1-77229-006-6 (bound)

I. Title. II. Title: Dove batte il cuore. English.

PZ7.T6Wh 2016   j853'.92   C2015-906590-9

Originally published in Italian in 2013 by Kite Edizioni,
as *Dove batte il cuore*.

Manufactured in Korea.
Book design by Heather Lohnes.

10 9 8 7 6 5 4 3 2 1

where the heart is♡

satoe tone

SIMPLY READ BOOKS

"Come with me,"
said the black cat
to the white cat.

"I'd like to catch these lights in the water and give them all to you."

The black cat tried to catch the lights,
but he couldn't. He tried with a leaf.

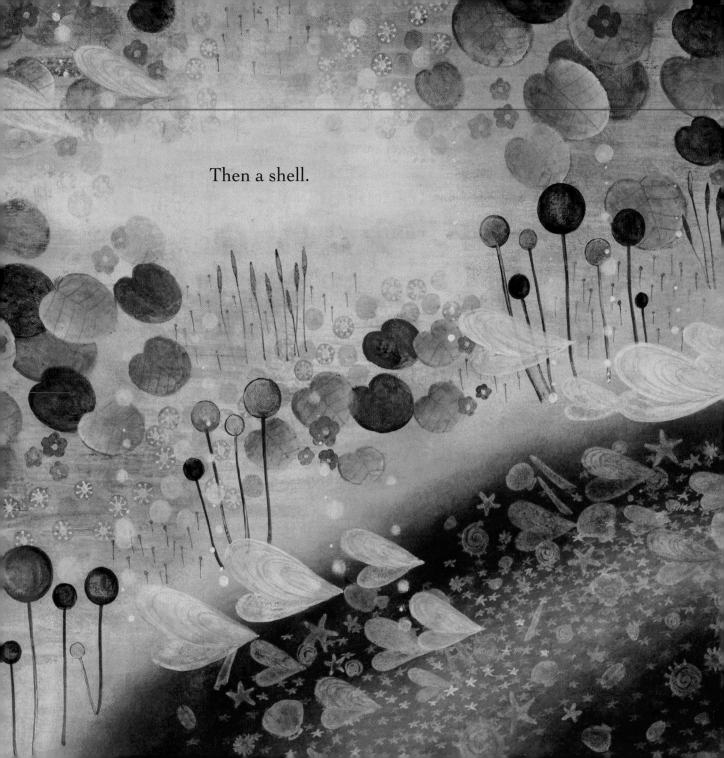

Then a shell.

He caught a jellyfish
in a bucket,
but it got away.

Then he caught a fish.

With his net he caught an
enormous, turbulent octopus.
But no lights.

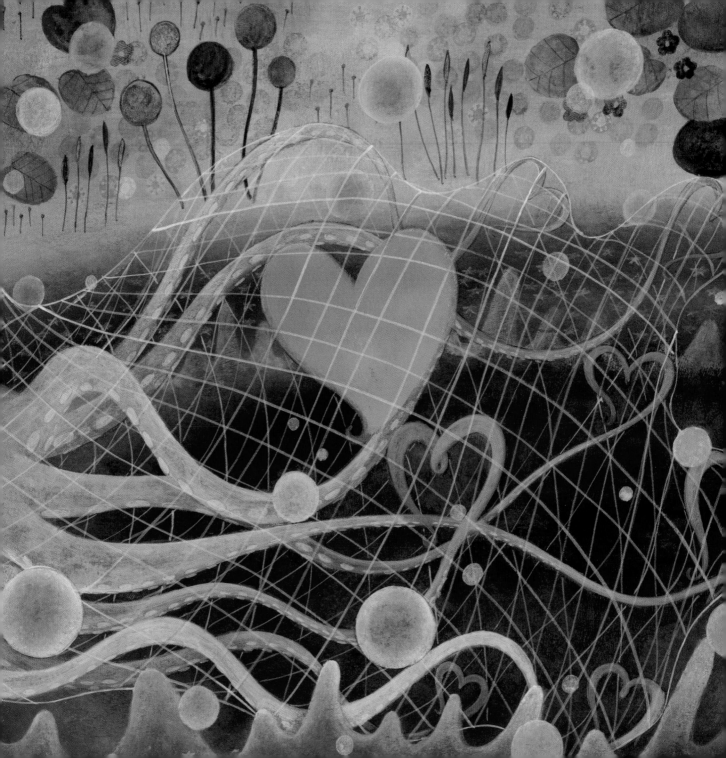

He decided to dive
in to find them.

But underwater it was cold and dark,
and he couldn't see a thing.

So the black cat came back up.
He was wet and miserable.
"They aren't there," he said.

But the white cat
touched his shoulder.
"Look."

The lights were in the sky.
Not in the water.

"They're beautiful," whispered
the white cat to the black cat.

He smiled. "All for you,"
he whispered back.

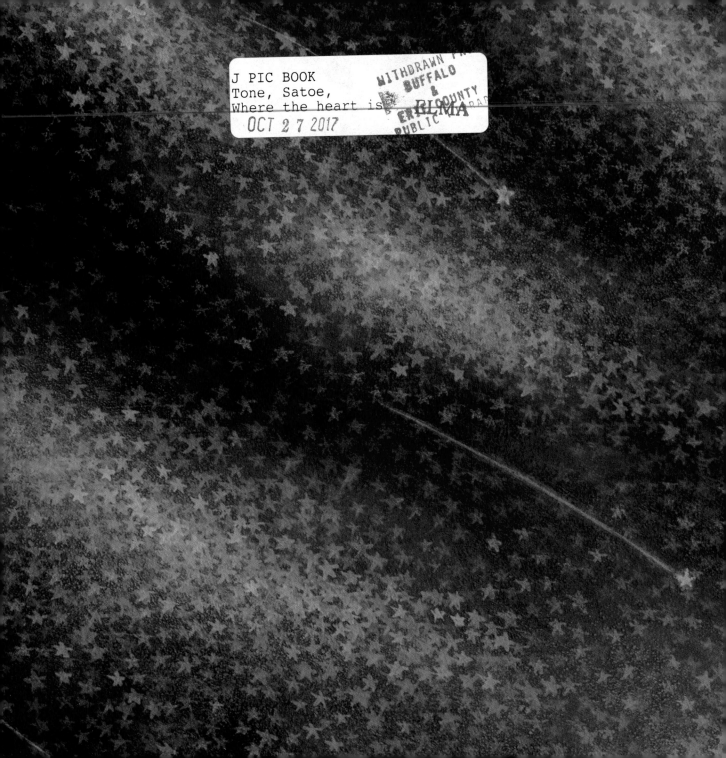